Grump Goes Galumphing

It's not very warm in the Ice Age but that's not why Grump's always so bad-tempered. No one seems to like him although he's so clever. He's always inventing things – even if they're not quite the things he was thinking of. And Herman helps him. Herman even likes him. But with friends like Herman, that terrible cloth-eared monster, who needs enemies?

DEREK SAMPSON

Grump Goes Galumphing

Illustrated by Simon Stern

A Magnet Book

With affection to
'Martha' Mary Digby

First published in 1986
by Methuen Children's Books Ltd
This Magnet edition first published in 1987
by Methuen Children's Books Ltd
11 New Fetter Lane, London EC4P 4EE
Text copyright © 1986 Derek Sampson
Illustrations copyright © 1986 Simon Stern
Printed in Great Britain by
Richard Clay Ltd, Bungay, Suffolk
ISBN 0 416 07202 X

Contents

1
Grump's Spring Picnic

'Maggots and mushrooms! Why doesn't anyone like me?'

Grump sighed and kicked at a stone. He was standing on a hilltop overlooking the lake and he looked very odd, like a scarecrow gone wrong. His arms and legs stuck like white knobbly sticks from the raggedy fur jacket that just covered his thin wobbly body. On his feet were even more ragged fur shoes. Warm feet were important if, like Grump, you lived in the Ice Age. Usually it was cold enough to chill the socks off a dancing bear.

'Not today, though,' said Grump. 'Today it's as warm as a fresh pancake.'

He sighed again. On the shore below everyone was having a marvellous picnic. Normally the Ice Age people were much too busy keeping warm and finding food to have fun, but today was different. Today was a really warm Spring day, and everyone had jostled from the caves where they lived on to the nearby beach to have a good time.

'Look at them playing games and having grubsome food! But nobody wants ugly old Grump along.'

He sighed a third time. All of his life the other cave people had mocked him, just because he was even shorter and funnier looking than they were. No wonder he had long ago taken to living in a cave by himself, and was just as lonely and grumpy as his name sounded.

'Well, if they don't want me along I . . .'

Grump stopped grumbling. Something warm and wriggly as a large worm was crawling over his hair and whiffling gently behind his ear. He knew that something only too well!

'Go away, bat ears!' he cried. 'No wonder nobody wants me with YOU around!'

He glared at the thing that was ruffling his hair. It was a trunk, a mammoth's trunk, and it belonged to the biggest, most cheerful animal that ever lived. Herman was his name, and like all Ice Age mammoths he looked like an elephant wearing his Sunday-best fur coat.

'Stop it! Stop whiffling round me like a mad vacuum cleaner.'

Grump sighed again – he was doing a lot of sighing that day. It was bad enough to be disliked by all of the other cave people, but to be liked so much by this big good-tempered creature was enough to make him chew his own toes in annoyance. It was no use, though. Herman never seemed to mind whatever he said or did.

They stood and looked together at the picnic below. The women were chattering and preparing food. The men were chattering and doing very little. The children were chattering and playing games, fun games like Caveman's Knock and Pass the Turtle and Blind Bear's Bluff. Grump glanced at Herman. The mammoth's large eyes were glistening with interest, and suddenly Grump grinned.

'Interested, tin tusks?' he asked. 'Like to play, too?'

It was naughty of Grump, but then he was a very naughty caveman. Now was his chance, he decided, to have some fun and, at the same time, get rid of a certain bothersome mammoth for a while.

'So what's it to be, my nutty chum?' he asked the eager mammoth. 'What shall we play?'

The difficulty was finding party games that he and Herman could play. Pass the Turtle was good for a time, and so was Doddling

Dinosaurs, but they could hardly play Leap-frog together. Grump tried to imagine Herman leaping over him, and shuddered. He could end up as a caveman flat enough to be posted under a door!

It did not matter, though. He was waiting for a chance to play one important game, and soon the moment had come. He took a strip of coney rabbit skin from inside his coat and waved it at Herman.

'Right, tatty tail,' he said, 'I'll blindfold myself with this and then try to find you.'

Herman did not understand what Grump was saying, of course, but he soon saw the idea of the game and thought it was splendid. He backed, he skittered, he whirled, and all of the time he made noises to lead the blindfolded Grump on. Once he even led him through a flock of squatting dodoes, who rose and waddled indignantly away to avoid their dancing feet.

'Where are you, oh mighty mammoth?' Grump called. 'You're much too smart for me, bulge brain.'

Grump was being cunning. He wanted Herman to lead him well away from the hilltop and the picnic below it before . . .

'Got you!' Grump shouted as he grabbed Herman's tail. 'Now it's your turn to be

blindfolded.'

Herman thought that being the blind-folded chaser was even more fun than being the leader. His caveman companion was so clever, always making noises close at hand, but always just out of reach, leading him on and on. He could have played the game for hours!

'But now it's over,' Grump giggled quietly to himself. 'Now it's goodbye to mousebrain for a long time.'

They were by a river, not the river that swept into the lake by the caves, but a wider, gentler one. It wound slowly for miles to a distant lake Grump knew. Often it was frozen hard, but now in the Spring ice-floes were

11

breaking away and floating downstream. It was them that Grump was watching.

'That one will do,' he breathed. 'Big enough to last a hairy lumper for miles.'

A few more noises and he had lured the blindfolded mammoth to the middle of the ice-floe and nipped ashore. Herman was still standing there, listening for where Grump might be, when the floe started to drift lazily away. He looked so happy, so trusting, that for a moment Grump felt a pang of guilt. He grunted and scrunched up his face.

'It's his own fault for badgering me! Anyway, he'll be safe, though it'll take him ages to

find his way back.'

Even so, he watched Herman safely out of sight before turning away. Then the mammoth was forgotten. Grump was eager to see what was happening at the picnic.

He and Herman had come a long way during their games, and soon Grump found himself running to get back quickly. What's more, he found himself dodging over many churning charging streams that had not been there before. He stopped.

'Funny,' he said, 'the river into our lake doesn't usually come this way? What's happened to it?'

When he arrived back at the hilltop, he quickly saw what had happened, and the sight sent his toes icy with horror. Trees carried by the melting snow had piled in the spot where the river usually tumbled downhill into the valley and blocked it completely! Now the water was trying to find an easier way to go. It was slowly making a new river oozing towards the edge of the hill nearby.

Grump raced there. Directly below the cave people were still enjoying their picnic, cheerfully unaware that the biggest waterfall ever would soon fall on them.

'They could all be drowned!' Grump gasped. 'But what can I do? No use shouting – they never listen to me!'

There was only one thing to do. Somehow he had to clear that log-jam. He ran back there and gazed at it in dismay. It was hopeless! He could never move all those trees. If only he had that idiot mammoth with him now!

'He'd soon move it all with his silly tusks. But I don't have tusks, so what can I use instead?'

Beside him was a long branch. If he could use it to push things upwards, just as Herman did with his tusks . . .

Grump tried it, and it worked perfectly. He put one end of the branch under the front log, heaved at the other end and . . . away it went! A moment later and water, logs, rocks, and one small caveman were cascading into the valley below. Grump was terrified at first, but soon started to enjoy it. He found that by using his long branch he could balance on a log as it was swept along. It was a very exciting feeling, and he was quite sorry when his log slid to a halt by the picnic party.

'Hallo, everybody!' he called chirpily. 'This is fun, isn't it? Did you see the way I moved the logs with this pole?'

Nobody spoke. Instead, they all stood glaring at him, and as he looked about him

Grump saw why. The water he brought down had surged over the shore. Now food, toys, and clothes bobbed soggily in the shallows. The picnic was ruined.

'But . . . but it wasn't my fault,' he protested. 'It would have been far worse if it had fallen from up there!'

He pointed to the cliff above them, but nobody took any notice. They did not know that Grump had saved them from a deluge, perhaps drowning. They only knew that he had apparently spoilt their picnic with one of his silly Grump tricks. They gathered their things resentfully, turned, and plodded away towards the caves.

Grump was almost dancing with impatience. 'You silly bonkers, I did it . . . I . . . well, it . . . Oh, what's the use!'

As he stood there, waving his fists like two flags in a high wind, he felt something like a large worm whiffling at his ear. He stopped. It was the second time that day that he'd had that feeling.

'Why, you cunning old cruncher, you got off that floe after all!'

He turned. Sure enough, Herman was standing behind him, hopefully waving a strip of rabbitskin from the end of his trunk. Grump wanted to be angry, he tried to be angry, but suddenly he was tremendously glad inside.

'Want some more games do you, tusker?' he demanded. 'Well, I've got nothing better to do . . .'

So, for the rest of the day, as they sat looking out over the lake, the cave people heard something very unusual. They heard Grump's laughter, high and happy, as he and Herman capered together in the warm sunshine, having a long long Spring picnic, all of their very own . . .

2
Grump's Colour Bucket

'Red apple, green apple, brown apple, blue,
Rainbow, rainbow, I love you.
Red apple, blue apple, brown apple, green,
Loveliest thing I've ever seen . . .'

Grump was singing, if you can call making a noise like a cow with its head in a bucket singing. He was also dancing, darting in circles and suddenly leaping into the air, grabbing at the sky with both hands. Every time he came down again he looked at his hands and groaned with disappointment.

'Blooming things, I'll never catch anything with them! They leak.'

He sighed. It had seemed such a good idea when he had woken that morning and looked glumly about his cave. Everything was so grey! Grey walls, grey clouds outside, even the toes peeking at him from the end of his bed were grey. That's when he decided that he needed some colour to brighten up his home.

17

'But nothing's bright round here,' he complained. 'Even the flowers turn brown as soon as you pick them.'

He was still pondering the problem when he left his cave and suddenly saw the answer above his head. There, shining in the sky not far from the lake, was a rainbow, a beautiful rainbow.

'That's it!' he cried. 'A lump of rainbow and I could paint my walls with it.'

Grump was being silly, of course. Even if he jumped as high as the moon he could never have grasped a rainbow, but he was a very obstinate little caveman. From that moment he hardly stopped leaping and grabbing, dancing and singing.

'Red apple, green apple, blue apple, brown,
Reach right up and pull you down.
Green apple, blue apple, brown apple, red,
Hang you up beside my bed.'

With those last words Grump made an especially high leap, certain that he would come to earth with a handful of rainbow colours. He didn't, nor did he come down to earth. Instead he landed on something hard and knobbly and furry. He looked down. He was sitting astride Herman's head!

'How did you get there, trundle toes?' he demanded. 'Kindly remove your brainbox from under me!'

Herman made no noise in reply; he was much too busy wondering what had happened. A few moments before he had found a nest of ants, and ants fascinated Herman. They were small and busy and self-important, always hurrying to and fro carrying bits of things. He had been so intent on following them, head low to the ground, that he had arrived accidentally under Grump.

'Here, mind what you're doing, bone-shaker. You'll have me off!'

Herman shook his head and Grump panicked, snatching at the mammoth's ears and dragging them over his eyes. Herman was now completely confused. One second he had been placidly trailing ants, and the next he was suddenly blinded, with a loud wriggly object on his head. He set off at a gallop, Grump clinging on desperately.

'Watch out, you'll have us in the lake, and I'm not due for a bath for months yet!'

The other cavemen were by the lake fishing. At least, they were trying to fish. Lately the fish had become too clever to take the bait from their lines and nobody was catching anything. So naturally they were not pleased when Herman skidded to a halt in

their midst.

Herman had glimpsed the lake at the last moment. He stopped. Grump didn't. With a wail of despair he whirled like a great spider over Herman's head into the water. After a lot of splashing and moaning he stood up. The cavemen stood up, too, waving their fists at him.

'What are you doing, crabface?' one shouted. 'You've ruined our fishing!'

'Come here and I'll use your bottom for bait!' another bellowed.

Grump was not listening. He was staring in wonder at the water around him. The rainbow was reflected in the lake, broken into a thousand colours by the ripples caused by his fall.

'It's down here as well as in the sky,' he breathed. 'I can reach down and just scoop the colours from the water.'

Even as he reached down the reflected colours vanished. He paused, frowned, then looked upwards. The sky was grey again. The rainbow was no more. He frowned for a moment longer, then suddenly grinned and banged his hands together.

'Of course, I know a place where there's always a rainbow! I can catch one any time!'

He was so entranced with his wonderful new idea that he was skipping as he left the lake. He paused by the cavemen, crossed his eyes, waggled his ears, and poked out his tongue at them before running off. They did not chase him. They were far too worried about their fishing to care about a cheeky caveman.

Herman did care, though. Now that he knew that it was Grump he had tossed into the lake, he was most worried about him. The small caveman seemed to be acting even more oddly than usual. Herman decided that he would have to keep an eye on Grump, and turned to plod in his footsteps.

'Ha ha! Now let's see what I can do with my

new colour bucket!.'

Grump came capering from his cave that afternoon. Around his head he was whirling his colour bucket, a large sack that he had made from rabbitskins, with long creepers at the sides as handles. He was very pleased with himself.

'Oh, what a clever lugs I am! With this I can scoop any rainbow out of the water.'

There was no time to waste if he were to have his cave painted in rainbow colours that day, and it was a long way to the place where he could always find a rainbow. Grump set off at a sharp trot. He was too busy to notice that there was always a mammoth just behind him, sidling from rock to rock like a huge but very shy ghost.

'And here I am,' Grump announced at last, 'the place where there's always a rainbow.'

He was lying on the edge of a cliff beside a thin waterfall that dropped into a pool far below. Cliffs almost completely circled the pool, so that it was dark and mysterious, and above it spray filled the air. That was why a rainbow always hovered in a shining crescent over the mountains at that point.

'And there it is again, down in the pool,' Grump chuckled. 'I'll just lower my colour bucket and lift it out'.

22

Slowly, carefully, he lowered his bucket by its handles to where the rainbow was reflected in the pool. The rainbow disappeared for a second as the bucket went under the water, then reappeared right in the centre of the bucket.

'Caught it!' Grump shouted in triumph. 'Right, heave away, my handsome fellow!'

That's when Herman appeared on the scene.

He had found a gap at the bottom of the cliffs and was by the edge of the pool. Like Grump he saw the rainbow in the bucket, but he could see something else, too – Grump's reflected face, seemingly underwater in the bucket. Herman did not hesitate. He could not let his favourite drown! He plunged his head into the water.

'Hey, what are you doing, flobberchops?' Grump shouted. 'Stop trunking my colour bucket to bits!'

Too late! The bucket was already fixed over Herman's head, filling his eyes with water and alarming him even more. It took only a minute for him to shake the thing from his head, but in that time his tusks had ripped holes everywhere in it. He was still glaring at it resentfully when suddenly it was whisked upwards out of sight. He looked up and saw

23

Grump's indignant face.

'See what you've done, cloth-head? You've ruined it, you terrible tusker!'

Herman did not understand what had happened. Somehow Grump had got out of the water and up on the cliff. It was all very puzzling for a well-intentioned mammoth. He turned and lumbered off, leaving Grump examining his bucket ruefully.

'It's more like a net than a bucket now,' he moaned. 'I'll never catch anything in this.'

Just to prove the point, he tossed the tattered bucket down into the pool and hauled it up again. Water spurted from every hole.

Grump groaned. No rainbow could ever be caught in it now! He was right. When he looked inside there were no gay colours. There were five fat fish instead!

'The water got out but they couldn't. But that means . . . oh, crusted crumbs, I've found a new way to catch fish!'

The cavemen were still sitting glumly over their fishing lines by the lake that evening when they heard, once more, a noise like a cow with its head in a bucket. They scowled at each other. That wretched Grump was around, and he was trying to sing again!

'How I wish wish wish
I had some fish fish fish
Upon a dish dish dish
For my tea . . .'

Grump stopped beside them looking so smug that they could have squashed him. They were about to rise to do just that when he poured a silver torrent of fish at their feet from his colour bucket.

'For you, chaps,' he announced. 'I'll show you my new way of catching fish tomorrow, if you're nice to me.'

He gave them a big smile, then walked on, swinging his bucket cheerfully. Life could be good for an ugly caveman sometimes. Perhaps now the other cave people would respect him a little more. Perhaps, also, he told himself, he might forgive a certain mammoth for ruining his colour bucket. After all, through that he had learned his marvellous new invention.

He heard a noise and looked behind him. Two large hopeful eyes were gazing at him from over a nearby rock. Grump grinned.

'All right, you hairy wardrobe, you can come to my cave. It's fried fish for all tonight!'

And so that night man and mammoth slept side by side, close to a flickering fire, whose light fell on the cave walls and made a thousand dancing rainbows of its own.

3
Grump's Little Outing

'Outside your caves, everyone! Spring-cleaning time!'

The voice that rang outside the caves that morning sent birds squawking into the air in alarm and icicles tinkling on trees. Everyone groaned and tried to snuggle deeper into bed.

'Come on, look lively! I'll make a sandwich of the last person here!'

Nobody ignored the voice after that. It came from Martha, the biggest, most fierce, of all the cave people. One look from her turned any sensible person's knees to jelly. In a flash, everyone scrambled from bed and lined up outside the caves. Martha strode up and down inspecting them.

'Someone's missing,' she growled. 'If it's that little demon Grump, I'll . . .'

She turned, just too late to glimpse Grump scuttering into place at the end of the line. Living in the farthest cave, he had been the last to hear her voice, but when he did he had moved like a runaway rocket. Now he waited, quaking, as Martha told everyone their jobs.

'You tidy the caves, and you polish the spiders' webs. You dust the rocks top and bottom, and you . . .'

She paused before Grump. He was the smallest, most trembly, of all the nervous cave people, yet there was something about him that always made Martha uneasy. As a result she was fiercest with him and gave him the worst jobs.

' . . . and you,' she said, 'can take my dear son Trug for a little outing.'

Grump's jaw dropped. Take Trug for a walk! He was the cheekiest and most mischievous of all the cave children, and being Martha's son meant that nothing on earth scared him. Taking him for a walk was as sensible as eating a bomb for breakfast!

'Please,' Grump protested, 'let me clean the crocodile's teeth instead!'

His voice faded. Something about the way that Martha was looking at his ears said that she was thinking of tying them in a neat knot over his head. Grump was very proud of his ears – they were good ears, splendid ears – and he wanted to keep them intact.

'All right,' he said gloomily, 'I'll do it.'

Shortly afterwards, he trudged dolefully

away from the caves, Trug skipping beside him. Grump's ears were burning, partly from the memory of what Martha might have done to them, but mainly from shame at having given in to her. He knew very well what the other cave people were thinking about him.

'They think I'm a cowardy custard for letting her bully me, even though they're as scared of her as I am. It's not fair!'

Right then, however, he had a worse worry. Trug was suspiciously cheerful, and a cheerful Trug meant only one thing – trouble!

'Let's find an octopus and tie its legs in knots, Grump!' he brightly suggested.

Grump shuddered. 'Let's just try staying alive, shall we?' he replied.

'At least your furry chum's along,' Trug continued chirpily. 'He'll be some fun.'

Grump look back and whimpered. A familiar figure was slodging through the snow in their footsteps, eyes wide and ears pricked with interest. Herman was on the trail again.

'Buzz off, you nosey dozer!' Grump cried, flapping his hands, 'I've got enough troubles looking after this mad elf.'

Herman stopped and pretended to examine a spring flower, stirring the fragile petals with a busy trunk. Then he sidled after them once more, certain that Grump would not hear him. Grump heard him perfectly well, but could not be bothered to stop again.

'Besides,' he muttered, 'even old tootle boots can't make things worse. It's going to be a dreadful day!'

Grump was right. That day with Trug was like having a tiger by the tail. If there was any sort of mischief the boy found it. He fell into rivers, threw rocks at dozing woolly rhinoceroses, and once even tried to use a snoozing snake as a catapult. After a few hours, Grump was exhausted.

'No more, Trug,' he pleaded. 'Must rest for a time.'

He collapsed beside a rock. It had been an awful day. He had been woken early by Martha's bawling, dragged over the countryside by her son, and now needed a doze. Oh, he knew it was foolish, knew that Trug would soon be up to something wicked, but he was too tired to care.

'Besides, old flop ears will watch him while I have a little kip.'

He opened one eye to check that Herman was standing patiently by, then closed it and fell asleep. He had a lovely sleep, and an even lovelier dream. In it he had just been voted the most popular caveman of the year and was

stepping forward for his prize when – he found he could not move!

'Strange,' he said, opening his eyes, 'feel like I'm tied up.'

He WAS tied up! A creeper was wound about his body and attached to something behind him. He craned his head backwards. He was tied to Herman's tail, and at the front end of the animal Trug was waving a honeycomb before Herman's hungry eyes.

'Here, munchy moo,' he was crooning, 'a little toothsome goo for a hardworking mammoth.'

Herman lurched forward. The one thing he could not resist in life was honey, and Trug knew it. He pulled the honeycomb just out of reach and Herman lurched again. Grump was dragged over a rock and bounced on the other side.

'Hey, mind out,' he cried desperately. 'I'm bumping on my bony bits!'

That was all he had breath to say in the next few minutes. In no time Herman was running, eyes bulging, trunk outstretched, trying to reach the honeycomb that Trug dangled before him. Trug was running, too, dancing through pools, over snowy ridges, across jagged glaciers, and all of the time Grump was dragged at the back like a piece of loose luggage.

'Never . . .oops . . .sit   down . . .ouch . . . again . . . ump!'

By the time all three of them tumbled into a snowfilled valley, Grump felt as if he were a thousand broken sticks held in an old sack. He lay there breathlessly for a moment, then wriggled free from his bonds and lifted Trug firmly by the ear.

'Right, Trug the Terrible,' he said grimly, 'this is when we go home.'

That was more easily said than done. They had come a long way, and there were no signposts or policemen to direct them homewards. Besides, when they climbed from the valley they found that a thick Ice Age mist had blotted out the world around them.

'Which way do we go, Grump?' Trug's voice quavered a little, 'I...I don't like fog.'

Grump grinned. 'Not so chirpy now, are we? Well, don't worry, the honey muncher will see us home.'

Herman was quite happy now. He had the honeycomb and was savouring every sweet drop of it. He did not mind one bit when Grump took his tail in one hand, took Trug's arm in the other one, and urged Herman to lead them home through the mist.

So they went on, Herman in the lead, pleased with his honeycomb; Grump next, pleased with his good idea; and Trug last, pleased to be doing something exciting.

None of them was pleased when Herman led them over the edge of a muddy slope.

'Whoops, I'm on a slippery dippery slide!' Grump wailed.

Normally the ground here was hard, but the thaw had turned it into the world's longest muddy helter-skelter. Mammoth, caveman, and boy, still linked together, whizzed downwards like an express train plunging off its rails.

'Right, at last we've got this place spick and span!'

Martha was addressing the weary cave people. They had been working under her fierce eye all day, and finally the clearing and caves were clean enough to please her.

They didn't stay that way long. Suddenly, in a shower of mud and rocks, three figures shot down from the hillside above the caves, skidded across the clearing, and stopped in a messy heap in a corner. Martha strode across, her eyes bonfires of fury.

'You've ruined our cleaning, you mad mudlark,' she roared at Grump. 'I'll mince you for this!'

Grump looked at her wearily. Normally he would have cowered from her anger, but not today. After the horrors Trug had put him through in the last hours nothing could scare him – not even Martha. He climbed to his feet and stared at her.

'Just try mincing me and see what happens, frying pan face!' he said coldly.

Everyone gasped. Grump's last moment had come for sure, they told themselves. Grump thought so, too, but to his amazement Martha's frown turned to a twitching smile. She backed away, rubbing her hands nervously.

'Of course,' she simpered, 'just a little joke. I'll clean up everything myself.'

All of his life Grump and the others thought that Martha backed away because Grump had at last stood up to her. They did not know that past Grump's shoulder she had seen a certain mammoth glaring at her – and something about Herman's fierce expression told her never again to bully his caveman friend. As it was, everyone gazed at Grump in amazed respect.

Then something else astonishing happened. Trug darted forward and tugged Grump's coat. 'Thanks for my outing, Grump,' he said, 'it was smashing.'

Grump nodded and turned towards his cave, his puny chest swelling with pride. Perhaps it had not been such a bad day. At least, that's what he told himself as he snuggled in bed later.

'Maybe I'm not a weedy helpless caveman after all,' he whispered contentedly. 'Maybe I'm a bit of a hero.'

Only Herman, lying in the darkness picking mud from his fur, knew any better. Only Herman knew . . . and he was not telling.

4
Grump's Big Bamboozle

'Put me down, trunk top! I'm not a silly sauce
bottle!'

Grump was upside down as he said those
words. Herman was grasping him with his
trunk by the ankles and shaking him firmly
but gently, as if trying to rattle the last penny
out of a money-box.

Herman continued to shake Grump for a little longer, then plonked him down in the deep snow. He gazed at the caveman sadly, shook his vast ears in disappointment, then lumbered off, looking rather sulky.

'Serves you right,' Grump shouted after him. 'You're nothing but a hairy pickpocket.'

Pockets, they were the trouble. Grump should never have invented them, but he had to do something to stop everyone stealing his things. He had made so many inventions, but the cave people seemed to think that they owned them. They were always popping into his cave when he was out to borrow a sharp flint or a well-bent boomerang.

'Not to mention mammoths stealing my new raspberry jam!' Grump bawled after Herman.

That was why he invented pockets, to hold his most precious possessions when he left his cave. He had made one mistake, though. At first he had kept snacktime goodies such as nuts and berries in them. Herman could smell a tasty munch in a caveman's pocket from a hundred yards away, and had taken to sneaking a crafty trunk in his pockets whenever the chance came.

39

'And shaking me upside down when he can't find any food. That chubby trunker thinks I'm a walking larder!'

Grump sighed. There was nothing for it, Herman would have to be taught a lesson. Not to hurt him, of course, but to teach him to keep his distance.

'It's like being chased by a big snuffling suitcase all of the time. Much more of it and I'll be a crazy caveman.'

Now it was just a question of finding Herman. That was easy. When he was not following Grump he usually took his midday nap on a small island out in the lake.

'And here he is, the snoozing beauty,' Grump chuckled. 'Well, he won't be snoozing long!'

Grump giggled as he crouched in a patch of bamboos at the lakeside, watching Herman snore peacefully on his little island. Somehow playing jokes on Herman always cheered him greatly. The difficulty was that the mammoth knew most of his tricks by now. He enjoyed them, too, but he liked to know when they were coming. That was why he slept somewhere where he could see all around him.

'The cunning tusker will know the moment I'm near,' Grump whispered, 'so what can I do?'

He sat down to think, then stood up quickly. He had sat on the sharp broken end of a bamboo plant and didn't think it was funny at all. Suddenly, he was grumpy again.

'Pesky thing!' he said, seizing the bamboo stick. 'I'll . . .'

He stopped. The stick was hollow inside. He could see right through it to where Herman slumbered. Grump's eyes widened and his pudgy nose wiggled in glee.

'What I can see through I can breathe through. The numb old noddlehead will never know I'm there!'

Herman was sleeping quietly, dreaming the dreams a mammoth dreamed in that long-ago world. Sometimes, however, he would raise his great head and look around him. There was nothing to see, no swimming cave-man, no drifting log or ice-floe that might conceal him. There was only the top of a bamboo stick poking from the water nearby. What was the harm in that? Herman went to sleep again.

Splurrff!

A jet of water hit Herman in the eye. He raised his head again, sharply this time. Nothing . . . not a thing around him. The lake was as peaceful as before. Perhaps there had been a sudden rain shower. He hummocked his shoulder and settled once more.

Under the water Grump giggled, at least, as far as someone breathing through a bamboo stick can giggle. He rose cautiously to the surface, took a mouthful of water, aimed the stick at Herman, and blew.

Splurrff!

Another jet of water hit Herman, and he opened his eyes. Another! They seemed to be coming from all directions! Confused and sodden, he look about for something to protect himself. The bamboo stick poking from the water! He seized it with his trunk, and with a mighty heave jerked it from the lake.

Grump was on the other end.

He should have let go, of course, but he didn't. Herman was the one who let go in

astonishment when he saw Grump above him. Stick and caveman soared through the air and crashed back into the lakeside bamboo patch.

'Bamboo bully! Caveman chucker!' Grump had picked himself up and was dancing in rage on the shore.

Herman shook his head. He did not know quite what had happened, but Grump did not seem to be hurt. In fact, he seemed his usual noisy angry self as he marched off, waving his bamboo stick indignantly. Herman flicked his trunk a time or two in puzzlement, then settled back to sleep.

Grump certainly was his old angry self, and he was angrier still when he arrived back at his cave. Someone was just coming out, carrying his precious tootle-horn.

'Here, what are you doing?' Grump demanded furiously. 'That's mine!'

'Not any more, weedy knees,' the intruder replied airily. 'I've decided that I want to learn to play it.'

Grump's mouth opened to protest some more, then stayed open in silent dismay. He suddenly realised that he was talking to Karva, the biggest bully of all of the cavemen. Nobody liked him, but nobody dared argue with him.

Karva smirked and strode away. 'Don't bother to ask for it back, beetle bonce,' he sniggered. 'From now on it's mine!'

Grump was near to tears. He had lost his game with Herman, lost his dignity, and now he had lost his darling tootle-horn. It was really too much! And when he saw the mess Karva had made of his cave . . .

'That does it!' Grump cried. 'From now on nobody comes in here. Not caveman, not mammoth, not nobody!'

It was the bamboo stick in his hand that gave him the idea. It was hollow but strong, and if he had more like it he could make a splendid door that would keep even the strongest person from his home. Quick as a blink, he was running back towards the bamboo patch.

'There, almost finished. Let's see someone try to squeeze through THIS!' Grump chuckled.

He was making a grand job of his door. Using a big stone, he banged the bamboos he had collected into cracks above and below his doorway. Soon he had a barrier that only a starving mouse could have squeezed through. Not until it was finished did he realise that he had forgotten something.

'Nobody can get in . . . but I can't get out

I'll be trapped in here for ever.'

Trapped he was. No matter how hard he tugged and strained at the bamboo bars, they would not budge. Eventually he collapsed, exhausted and miserable, inside his prison. He was still lying there when a bright voice spoke.

'What's up, Grump? Are you starting a zoo or something?'

Grump looked up in sudden hope, then down in defeat. It was only Trug grinning at him through the bars, and he was not strong enough to pull out the bamboo. It needed somebody strong, as strong as . . . a mammoth! All at once, Grump was hopeful again.

'Trug,' he said winningly, 'would you fetch Herman for me?'

Trug looked cunning. 'What'll you give me if I do?'

Grump groaned. Children were so greedy nowadays! Then he noticed a bamboo stick by his feet and his eyes narrowed. Perhaps other things than water could be blown through it – pebbles, for instance. He scrambled to his feet and whispered to Trug through the bamboo bars.

'Trug,' he said, 'Karva bullies you, doesn't he? Would you like to get your own back?'

As he whispered on, Trug's grin grew into a wicked smile. A minute later the boy ran off, and ten minutes after that he returned with Herman strolling placidly beside him. The mammoth looked at the bamboo door, curled his trunk round it, gave one wrench, and it was in pieces.

'I'm free!' Grump shouted, capering in the bright air. 'Free as a cloud!'

It was a very contented caveman who lay by his fire that night. Yes, people could still come into his cave and take what they wanted, but what did he care?

'Let them come if they want! Let Karva come, the poor old thing.'

In a cave nearby Karva was trying to play

Grump's tootle-horn but not doing very well. Every time he blew a note there was the whizz of something flying through the air, and he would yell as if a bee had stung him. Grump smiled. Trug was out there in the dark, taking revenge for both of them.

'Here, gumchops,' Grump said, 'have some more raspberry jam.'

He held out a shell filled with jam to the snuffling trunk of Hermàn, who lay sleepily beside him. After all, the mammoth deserved some reward for helping Grump to invent the world's first pea-shooter.

5
Grump's Violin

'Lummy looby, I'm so bored I could burst! I'd have more fun tickling a snail with a feather.'

Grump groaned like a ghost with toothache and looked about him discontentedly. He was all alone, sitting outside the caves. There was nothing to see and nothing to do. Even Herman was away somewhere on private mammoth business, so there was nobody to tease, either. Life was very tedious.

'And I can't play my tootle-horn because that bully beast Karva stole it. Oh, my!'

He had tried everything to amuse himself – crossing his eyes and trying to touch his nose with the tip of his tongue, flapping his ears to attract passing butterflies, and just lying back and watching specks of dust float across his eyeballs. Nothing had worked. He was still bored.

'Might as well see how the others are getting on,' he muttered, getting to his feet.

He trudged into the forest. All of the cave people were there today, preparing a special clearing in the trees for a dance to be held in two days' time. It was a very important dance to celebrate the first full moon of the Spring, and everyone was invited, even Grump.

'Except they only want me there to bang my log drum and blow my tootle-horn so as they can dance. They . . .'

He stopped in sudden dismay. His tootle-horn! How would he play it at the dance if Karva had stolen it? And if the bully should steal his drum, too, Grump would not be needed at all! Suddenly he was running through the trees, his heart pattering as quickly as his feet.

'I knew it, that sneaky cave stealer has snitched my log drum too!'

Grump's wail sounded like a parrot cry in

the forest clearing where the cave people were preparing for the dance. There, on a large flat rock in the centre, Karva was standing as proud as a prince. In one hand he had Grump's tootle-horn and in the other he held a heavy stick with which he banged on Grump's log drum beside him.

'But you can't let him play instead of me!' Grump cried in despair. 'It's just not fair!'

The cave people looked up from their work, shrugged, and looked away. Nobody was going to argue with Karva if he wanted to play Grump's things. Besides, there was so much to do. The women were decorating the trees with garlands, the men were arranging boulders for seating, and the children were cheerfully raising clouds of dust while pretending to sweep the floor. Grump looked at them glumly.

'Oh, what's the use?' he moaned. 'Nobody likes me! They don't care if I play at the dance or not.'

He turned and walked away into the dark forest, his bony shoulders sagging. It was so hard being a little caveman that nobody cared about. To be a . . .

Plop!

Something large and round and hollow landed on Grump's nose, rested there for a moment, then exploded like a watery bomb. He staggered back. Plop! Plop! Plop! More of the things were swirling about him, all popping and showering him with dampness.

'What's happening? I'm being bombarded with bubbles!'

At that moment he saw a trunk, wavering like a giant grey hosepipe, pointing from over a nearby bush, and all at once he knew just what was happening. A certain mammoth was up to mischief again!

'Why, you barmy bubble blower, attack me would you?' Grump shouted.

He tried to sound angry, but he couldn't. He could not even feel sorry for himself any more. No matter how much everyone disliked him, Herman was always around, anxious to have fun with him. Somehow that made Grump want to laugh.

'Right, flop chops,' he called, 'if it's a bubble battle you want, I'm ready!'

He dodged around the bush. Herman was there, eyes twinkling, trunk dipped into a greasy pool for more slodgy water to make bubbles. Grump reached into his pocket for a lump of the rubbery stuff he had once found oozing from a tree. This time he would be ready!

It was a good battle they had that after-

51

noon. Herman tried to soak Grump with a stream of bouncing bubbles blown from his trunk. Grump fought back by stretching his rubber lump and whanging the bubbles to bits before they reached him. They might have gone on for hours but Herman cheated by seizing the end of the rubber with his trunk when it flicked near him.

'Watch out, you'll have me over, you humpy buffoon!'

Grump braced himself and pulled at his end of the rubber. Herman pulled his. Gradually it stretched tighter and tighter into a taut rope. Then, when it seemed ready to break, they accidentally scraped it against an

overhanging branch. A strange howling sound came from it. They stopped, blinked, and scraped it again. Again the same howling noise. Herman was so astonished that he released his end of the rubber rope, sending Grump toppling backwards. The little caveman hardly noticed. He was much too interested by what had happened.

'If you stretch this stuff and rub a stick across it you get a sound like music,' he breathed.

Herman was always puzzled by the things Grump did, but what happened next amazed him. Muttering excitedly to himself, Grump stretched the rubber rope along a stout stick

and scraped another stick across it. Sure enough, the strange musical note came. What's more, when he made the rope tighter or slacker different notes came. The very idea sent Grump jigging in delight.

'Who wants a boring log drum or tootle-horn?' he chortled. 'Wait until they hear THIS at their silly old dance!'

Nobody saw Grump in those next two days as he learned to play his new musical instrument, his violin, deep in the forest. Nobody but Herman heard him, either. That's not quite true. Other animals were there, peeping from behind trees, heads cocked, eyes glittering, fascinated by the weird noise from his violin. Grump did not notice. He was far too busy practising.

'And now,' he announced eventually, 'I'm ready. Grump the great violinist is off to the dance!'

The dance was in full swing when Grump arrived. He watched quietly from the clearing's edge, hugging himself with glee. Karva was there on the flat rock, banging the drum, blowing the tootle-horn, and looking very tired with the effort.

'And won't he be sick when he hears my marvellous new invention,' Grump giggled to himself.

The dancing stopped, and Grump's moment had come. Bracing his thin body, he strode towards the flat rock, jumped on it in front of Karva, and faced the dancers.

'Ladies and gentlecavemen,' he told them, 'I will now sing a song and play on my new violin.'

Everyone agreed afterwards that Grump's song was not a bad one, even sung in his squeaky voice. What nobody could bear was the sound of his violin. It was awful, like having a hundred hungry wolves howling in your head. It ws so painful that nobody had the strength to interrupt his song.

'Though dodos are delightful
And dinosaurs are fine
And make a tender biteful
When you sit down to dine,
The way to make me grateful,
If I should eat with you
Is to serve a steaming plateful
Of tasty rabbit stew.'

Grump paused. He was rather pleased with that verse, and was about to launch into a second one praising the delights of onions and carrots and dumplings in rabbit stew, when he noticed something odd. His audience were looking past him, not at him, and in their eyes was fear, not pleasure.

He glanced backwards, and what he saw turned his toes clammy with terror. Grouped behind him on the rock like a monstrous choir, were twelve huge Ice Age wolves, their fangs gleaming in the firelight. Everyone was too scared to move, particularly Karva, who had an extra large wolf perched firmly on his chest. It was he who realised what had happened.

'Your . . . your violin,' he croaked, 'they like your violin. Play it again before they eat us all!'

Grump needed no urging. Desperately he put his stick across the rubber string of his violin and tried to play. But he was too trembly with fear to do it properly. The stick caught in the string, pulled back and back as Grump tugged, then whizzed away and hit a wolf in the eye. The animal shook its fierce head and fled into the night, howling indignantly. Grump gaped, then turned to the other cave people urgently.

'Quick,' he called, 'quick, give me more sticks!'

Sticks were thrust at him from all directions and fired from his violin as quickly as they came. Soon the forest was loud with the howls of fleeing wolves, until at last they were all gone. When he had finally stopped trembling, Grump smiled rather nervously at the other cave people.

'My . . . um . . . my violin's good for chasing away animals, isn't it?' he said.

'And for bringing them,' a caveman growled sourly. 'We could have all ended up in a wolf's tum!'

Grump looked at them hopefully for a second, then sighed and turned away. It was always the same! Whatever he did, whatever he invented, nobody appreciated him. He was just walking sadly towards the trees when a voice called to him.

'Hey, Grump, don't go! We need you to

play for us.'

Grump turned back. It was Trug, and he was pointing into the darkness. There, just visible in the moonlight, was Karva, scurrying towards the caves as fast as he could totter. Trug grinned and took Grump's arm.

'I think Karva's decided that it's too dangerous to play at our dances,' he said. 'Will you do it instead?'

Would he? Grump bounded onto the flat rock beside his beloved drum and tootle-horn. And he played them that night better than ever before, so that all agreed that it was the best dance ever. He didn't play his violin, though . . . not then.

He played it later, though, very quietly as he lay by his fire, his drum and tootle-horn at his side. He played it for a large animal just outside his cave, its trunk swaying slowly in time to the music.

'That's what I've always liked about Herman' Grump murmured in sleepy contentment. 'He's a very musical mammoth . . .'

6
Grump's Thin Ice

'Slippery nippers! They'll be sorry when their toes turn to icicles!'

There's no doubt about it, Grump was jealous. For once, an invention was not his. It was Trug who first tied thin strips of wood to his feet and slid over the ice on them. It worked splendidly. The strips soon wore out, but while they lasted he could whizz across the ice quicker than a dizzy duck. Soon everyone was on the frozen lake by the caves skating – everyone but Grump, that is.

'Don't want to! Who wants to be a whacky whizzer, anyway?'

He was sitting on a log by the lake, his elbows on his knees, his face resting on his knuckles like a crinkled apple balanced on two white sticks. He watched the skaters and tried not to look envious until he could bear it no longer.

'Got to go,' he announced. 'I'm a caveman with important things to do.'

He was lying. He had nothing more important to do than kicking fir cones or making ugly faces at rabbits. The truth was, he was too afraid of looking foolish to go on the ice.

'My body's not right for skating, that's the trouble. I go one way and my lolly legs go the other.'

He knew because he had tried, practising alone on a frozen pond high on the mountain. He trudged in that direction now, wishing just wishing, that for once there were something he could do really well. He was so glum that it was some time before he noticed a strange noise coming from the pond ahead of him.

'Whatever's that? It's a sort of whistling, scraping sound, like a whale cleaning its teeth.'

He ran forward and peered through the bushes at the pond, and suddenly he was not glum any more. Suddenly he was rolling in the snow and laughing, kicking and wriggling like a puppy with a worrisome itch.

'Why, that tatty tusker thinks he's the world's first skating mammoth!'

He peered again. Herman was on the pond, his tusks resting on the ice and his trunk stretched before him while his great back legs pumped vainly to try to push himself along. Herman had decided to try this skating business, and was making a very silly mess of it.

'Not that way, you wobbly wardrobe,' Grump cried derisively. 'Here, I'll show you.'

He tied on his wooden skates, stepped onto the ice, and promptly fell down. He blinked, grunted, struggled to his feet and fell down again. He did a lot of falling down and bouncing up in the next few minutes. In fact he did it so often that he looked as if he had springs fitted to his bottom somewhere. At last, however, he lay breathless and defeated.

'Can't stand up. Need some help.'

He craned his head hopefully towards

Herman. The mammoth had slithered ashore by now, and had no desire to go on the ice again, but he did want to help Grump. He paused for a moment, his brow wrinkling like an old blanket in thought, then snapped a creeper from a tree and tossed one end to the caveman.

'Clever mammoth, kind mammoth,' Grump crooned gratefully. 'Just let me get hold of it . . .'

He grasped the creeper and tottered to his feet. Herman tugged the other end gently and Grump sailed smoothly over the ice. His eyes widened. Suddenly, with Herman to help him, skating did not seem difficult at all.

'It's as easy as sucking custard! I'll get my hairy hauler to pull me around the pond a bit.'

Poor Herman had little rest for the remainder of that day. Patiently, he pulled this way and that as Grump clung to the creeper and learned to skate faster and faster. Soon the jubilant caveman did not need the creeper at all. Without it he could skate forwards and sideways, and sometimes even backwards though he did not mean to. At last he squadged to a triumphant halt in the snow at Herman's feet.

'See that, lobby lugs?' he crowed. 'I'll skate the socks off them on the lake tomorrow!'

The lake was crowded with skaters when Grump arrived next day, but he was not one bit nervous. He sat on a log, tying on his skates and giggling eagerly to himself.

'Just see that ice melt when I whizz along! My, won't they be impressed!'

Grump was right, everyone was impressed. Even Trug could not skate as well as he, or whirl around, or hold one foot in the air. It was when he started to show off that the trouble started. He was heading out across the open lake to show how fast he could skate when he realised one thing – he had not learned how to stop!

'Not unless there's a big pile of snow to catch me! What do I do now?'

He was going too fast to stop, speeding past a small island to where the ice ended in very cold, very wet, water, and jagged ice floes that would make mincemeat of him. He moaned and closed his eyes, just as something long and curly flipped out from the island and twisted about him.

'What's that? A creeper! But where? How?'

He looked towards the island. Herman was there, standing by the solitary tree, the end of the creeper firmly in his trunk. He had come to watch Grump, and naturally he had brought a creeper with him.

'Well done, wag nose!' Grump bellowed. 'Now just hold tight while I tug on this thing and stop!'

Grump pulled on the creeper, but it did not stop him. Instead, it swung him in a great curve around the island, back towards the shore and the other skaters again.

Nobody could agree afterwards quite what it felt like. Some said that it was like being swept up by the giant hand of some mad clock. Others claimed that it was more like being caught by a vast fishing net. One thing they all agreed on – it was most unpleasant. Grump's creeper, as he whizzed in a big

circle, snatched up the skaters one by one, so that by the time he was heading past the island again they were all clinging to it like pegs on a clothes line.

It was worse the next time round. The creeper got shorter as it wound about Herman, and the skaters jostled shoulder to shoulder, shouting and complaining. By the third time round they could not shout because they were jammed into a heaving parcel of human beings. Only Grump managed to bawl a frantic order to Herman.

'Let us go, you mad maypole! For goodness sake let us go!'

Herman obediently snapped the creeper. The human bundle whirled across the lake, spun a dozen dizzy times, then slid to a halt by the shore. It lay there groaning for a moment before Grump managed to wriggle free and look in horror at the damage.

'The lake's cracked everywhere. It's ruined for skating. They'll boil me in butter for this!'

He had intended to stay and sort out a leg or two from the struggling parcel of people beside him, but something told him that it would be wiser to leave. He hobbled ashore, tore the skates from his feet, and flung them far from him.

'Wretched things, it's their fault everything went wrong! Nobody will ever talk to me again after this.'

Grump had plenty of time for thinking of skates and suchlike in the next few days. He dared not return to his cave. Instead, he crouched by a small fire deep in the forest, deciding in his usual Grump way that nothing that had happened was one bit his fault!

'It was those teeny weeny skates. Now if I'd had long, wide ones, and poles to hold me up . . .'

So, because he had nothing better to do, he set about making special new skates. It took a long time, finding the right bits of wood, scraping them with his flint until they were flat and thin, then choosing stout poles to keep him upright. At last, however, he was ready.

'And when they see my new skates they'll

be so amazed that they'll forget all about how I cracked the lake!'

He was crouched, looking at his practice pond up the mountain. The cave folk were using it now since the big lake was ruined, so it was very crowded. That was why Grump was waiting. He wanted everyone to see his new skates when he slid on to the ice. They were splendid ones, wider than his feet and poking far out beyond his heels and toes, and in each hand he held a balancing stick.

'And there's a gap now, so here I go . . . o . . . o !'

It was a shame that Herman touched Grump's shoulder just then. The mammoth had not seen his favourite caveman for days and was worried about him, so when he saw Grump by the pond he reached out for a friendly pat – but a mammoth's pat is like a bang from a bus!

'Watch out, everyone! Watch out for the Great Grump express!'

Sped on by Herman's pat, Grump shot through the astonished skaters, across the pond, and disappeared down the snowy mountain on the other side. Everyone gaped at each other for a moment, then rushed to the edge to see what had happened to him.

'Showering snowballs, watch him whizz!'

Trug called in awe.

Grump's skates worked well on snow. He flashed down the hillside like a runaway rocket, spraying snowy plumes behind him as he steered with his poles around trees and over bumpy rocks. At last, however, he found a rock too big to slide over. He soared through the air, turned an interesting cartwheel or two, then landed upside down in the snow.

'Where am I? I'm in a million bits and they all hurt!'

Grump was sitting up, looking dazedly at the people gathered about him. They ignored him. They were far too busy examining his new skates.

'What do you call them, Grump?' Trug demanded. 'They're terrific.'

Grump tried to still his whirling head. He thought of the noise his skates had made on the snow and replied weakly: 'Skis . . . they're skis!'

Grump was right about one thing. Everyone was so pleased with his new invention that they forgot about boiling him in butter for ruining the skating lake. They even carried him home to his own dear cave and left him there before hurrying off to make skis of their own. He could hear their shouts and laughter in the evening air as he fell slowly to sleep.

'They're welcome to skis,' he murmured. 'Who wants to get all bruised and bumped, anyway?'

He was too tired to care. Besides, he could hear another sound outside his cave. It was the sound of a mammoth gently breathing as it kept guard. Herman was watching him, and somehow that made Grump feel glad.

7

Grump's Lonely Boat

'Brush and bubble! Brush and bubble!
Scrub away those grubby smears,
Clear the toes of rocks and rubble,
Don't forget behind the ears,
Do it once and do it double,
Never been so clean in years.
There, it's really worth the trouble,
What a handsome chap appears!'

Grump was having a bath. He was a very clean little caveman. Once a year without fail he took himself off to a warm pool and scrubbed himself all over. It was painful and unpleasant, but it had to be done. Today was different, however, today was special. It was only seven months since his last bath, yet here he was again, rubbing himself bright as a bubble.

'Must be clean and smart if I meet someone on my voyage,' he said, wincing a little as he touched his glowing skin.

He was out of his bath now, standing by a

quiet inlet by the lake. He was looking at his new boat. It wasn't so much a boat, really, more of a raft. It had taken ages to make, finding logs of the same length and binding them with creepers into a big platform. There was a pole at the back for steering and pushing himself along in shallow water, and even a small cabin where he could sleep.

'Magnificent! Those ugly old rumtuggers will pop with envy when they see it.'

Nobody had yet seen his raft – Grump had kept it as secret as a squirrel's nutstore – but now was the moment to launch it and startle the world with his cleverness.

'I name this ship Grump's Glory,' he announced to nobody in particular as he pushed it into the water.

It floated perfectly, and though it was awkward to steer with the pole and staggered across the lake from side to side like a crippled crab, Grump hardly noticed. He was much too proud of his new invention as he stepped ashore on the beach by the caves where a crowd of curious cavemen had gathered.

'What do you call that, stickle-legs?' one demanded, kicking the raft suspiciously.

Grump smirked. 'It's my new wonder boat. You can go anywhere on it without wetting your feet.'

'They'll soon get wet when the crocodiles chump you for breakfast!' another snorted.

They wandered off, giggling and nudging each other, but for once Grump was not hurt. Tomorrow he would leave their jokes behind forever.

'Because I'm sailing away and I'll never be badgered by bullying cavemen or pesky mammoths again!'

He snuggled down in his bed. Herman! Where was Herman? Somehow he wished that the mumbling monster were around so that he could tease him for one last time, but the mammoth was nowhere to be seen. Grump sighed, closed his eyes, and dreamed of the great adventure before him.

Herman was still missing when Grump had finished loading his raft next day. Everyone was missing. Nobody came to see him off – nobody, that is, unless you count a cheeky little cracker like Trug.

'Where are you going on that lump of logs, Grump?' he asked.

'Across the lake, down the river, and as far as I can go,' Grump replied loftily.

Trug giggled. 'In that case you'll probably tumble off the end of the world!' he announced cheerfully.

Grump shuddered. What if he really did fall off the end of the world? Then he told himself that it did not matter, anyway. Nobody would miss him. Even that badgersome mammoth beast had not bothered to come to see him leave.

He pushed the raft from the bank, and Trug ran a little way beside him along the lake shore. Grump did not look back, though. Somehow he felt foolishly that he might burst into tears if he did. He did not even look back when, as his raft was swept into the river beyond the lake, he heard Trug faintly shouting.

'Grump! Goodbye, Grump. You're awfully silly, but I like you.'

Grump frowned and shook his head. He must have misheard. Trug seemed to be shouting that he liked him, but that was im-

possible. Nobody liked him: that was why he
was leaving.

If he had looked back then he would have
seen that someone else had come to say goodbye. Herman was by Trug on the shore,
waving his trunk a little sadly. He did not
know where Grump was going, but he sensed
that something important was going out of his
life.

Grump looked firmly ahead. 'Goodbye and
good riddance to them all,' he murmured.
'I'm off – maybe off the end of the world.'

Grump did not fall off the world, but many times in the next days he thought that he was going to. His home was in the high mountains, and the river had a long journey down to the sea. It did it with terrifying downrushes and easy placid pools, and all of the time he had to keep his clumsy craft afloat. All of the time as well, as they left the high lands, it became hotter and hotter.

'Phew, it's so hot I'll probably melt and bubble away!' Grump moaned.

Eventually, all he could do was doze in his shady cabin as he drifted downstream. Strangely, he found himself dreaming of Herman and sometimes Trug. He could almost see them through his half-closed eyes and hear their voices.

Grump sat up in sudden alarm. There *were* faces looking at him, and voices, but not Herman's or Trug's! Two figures were standing over him. Strangers had boarded his raft!

'Please,' Grump stuttered, 'don't hurt me!'

The strangers grinned and reached towards him. Grump skidded back, his teeth almost popping out in terror. Then one patted his head and the other touched his arm, and Grump knew that he had nothing to fear from them. Still grinning, they helped him into the open air. Grump looked about him and was silent with wonderment.

Long afterwards, when he was an old old caveman, Grump would tell of the land he found himself in, but everyone would laugh and shake their heads and say that Grandpa Grump was telling enormous lies again.

Who could believe, they would say, in a land so warm that people had to wear hardly any clothes? Where trees had wide shady leaves and tasty fruits that you could just reach up and pick? Where there were grass houses instead of caves to live in? It was just too silly!

Grump could never make them believe it, but it was true.

From the day he arrived he never stopped being filled with wonder at the land and the people he had found. They were amazed at him too. Why did he wear heavy shaggy clothes, they asked? And why was his skin an odd pink colour instead of beautiful brown like theirs?

Grump did not resent their questions because – and that was the most wonderful thing of all – they liked him! They really liked him, and he was not Grump the outcast any more.

'No wonder I was a grumpy scrumper at home, everyone was so horrid to me, but here . . .'

There was so much to do, and Grump was so happy, that often he almost forgot how he had lived before . . . but not Herman, nobody could ever quite forget Herman. Sometimes in his dreams Grump would hear the mammoth's high, excited, tootling when they played together.

Even Herman would slip from his mind in the daytime. There was fishing on the warm sea in light boats driven by something called sails, and there were delicious fruits and nuts to be gathered from friendly trees. In the evening there were fires to sit around, and laughter, and stories to be told – such stories!

The stories were Grump's downfall. He was a stranger, so everyone was interested in what he had to tell, and naturally, being Grump, he . . . well . . . boasted a little.

'So I took this woolly rhinoceros,' he said, 'and tied a knot in its tail.'

He looked at his listeners. They were leaning towards him, eyes sparkling, fascinated. They knew nothing about large fierce animals and believed every word he was saying. Grump hugged himself with glee, and started speaking again.

'Then along came this sabre-tooth tiger, its fangs dribbling . . .'

Ggggraahhh! Mmmmyumph! Gggggraahhh!

Grump stopped talking, his hairs standing on end. Nobody stirred. They all looked towards the jungle nearby from where the dreadful noise had come, chilling their bones and setting the firelight swaying.

Gggggraahhh!

There it was again, worse this time! Something loud and horrible was trapped in the trees, crashing around and roaring as if ready to make a meal of the first person it met.

'What's that?' Grump asked his companions nervously, trying to stop his voice quavering. They shook their heads.

'We don't know,' one replied. 'We've never heard anything like it before.'

Grump looked at them closely. Oddly, nobody seemed as scared as he was. Some were actually smiling at him, and one small girl stepped forward and handed him a stick confidently.

'Here, Grump,' she said, 'you will deal with the fierce monster for us. You are a great brave huntsman!'

Grump gulped. Surely nobody expected him to go out alone into the dark to face whatever howling horrible creature was there?

'But I can't!' he protested. 'I've got a

headache and I . . .'

He stopped. They were still smiling at him, still certain that brave Grump could save them. He groaned. All of his life he had hoped for a home and friends like this. If he went into the jungle and met the monster he would lose it all for sure. If he did not, perhaps his new friends would not respect or like him any more.

Grump looked at them again, and suddenly he knew that being liked by these people was the most important thing in the whole world to him. He climbed to his feet, waved the stick, and smiled foolishly.

'Oh, well,' he said, 'say goodbye to one very silly little caveman!'

Then he turned and ran into the jungle, towards whatever faced him in the dark.

8
Grump's Hairy Helper

'Herman, you mouldy muddy mammoth, what are you doing here?'

Grump stood in the moonlight, a stick in his hand and amazement on his face. He had crept into the jungle expecting to be munched by a monster. Instead, in a muddy pool, wound round and round with weeds, he had found the world's biggest, hairiest parcel. It lay quiet now, two large eyes looking up at him.

'You followed me here just to be a nuisance, didn't you?' Grump demanded.

His voice was harsh, but he was not harsh inside. He said afterwards that he felt happy because he knew now that he would not be munched, but that was not it. He was happy to see Herman. He leaped into the pool and tugged the mammoth's ears in fierce joy.

'Stay here, loony lugs!' he ordered. 'We'll soon get you out.'

Ten minutes later Herman had been

hauled from the pool and was being washed down in the river. Children swarmed over him scrubbing his fur, his trunk, and peeking through his earholes to try to see each other. He adored it!

'That's enough or he'll shrink into a mouse,' Grump said at last. 'Bedtime!'

Herman slept in Grump's hut that night. It was a tight squeeze but the caveman did not mind. He did not even mind that the exhausted creature snored all night, lifting the grass sides of the hut with each blast of his trumpeting trunk. By morning Grump had slept hardly a wink, but he was still cheerful.

'Up you get, lumber chumps!' he ordered. 'I'll show you around.'

There was so much to show Herman, and somehow it all seemed better for Grump because the mighty creature was with him. They explored the village and the jungle, nosed along the seashore, and even went for a swim.

'It's quite safe here,' Grump explained. 'The sea's closed in a sort of small bay.'

He pointed across the water. Two cliffs curved out from the shore like crab's pincers, their points almost touching, but with a small gap through which the sea could tumble. Outside the cliffs the water was grey and troubled. Inside it was blue and calm.

'Come on, lazy boots,' Grump called, flopping into the water, 'last one in is a dinosaur's dinner!'

He stopped. Herman had not followed him. Instead, he was gazing at the clifftop in bright excitement, as if seeing an old friend. Puzzled, Grump gazed there, too, and saw something that he had never noticed before. At the tip of the cliff, overhanging the gap to the sea, was a huge rock. It was craggy and broken, yet there was something familiar about it. Then Grump realised what it was.

'It looks like a mammoth! But it's only a rock, you silly mophead. Come on, let's swim!'

He dragged Herman into the water, and as they played, the strange stony figure was forgotten. Everything was forgotten in noisy splashing fun.

It was all fun for them both in the next days, and when Grump was away, Herman had the children to play with. And if they were busy he could always go and stand by the stone mammoth and pretend it was real. Yes, it was fun. It was a shame that Grump had to spoil it all, even though he did not mean to.

The children had given Herman a hat of dried leaves to protect him from the sun. It was huge, round and flat, with a hump for his head, so that when he went out in it he looked like a strolling mushroom. Grump liked mushrooms, but he also liked mischief . . .

'One good hat deserves another,' he giggled from behind a bush.

Herman was walking in the sand, practising making ditches with his feet. He saw a hat on the shore before him, stopped, and touched his head with his trunk. His own hat seemed to be in place. Still, deciding that a

mammoth could never have too many hats, he reached for the hat on the sand. It moved. Herman blinked and reached again. The hat moved once more.

'The hairy hatstand, he'll never catch the thing!'

Grump was twisted with glee, kicking in silent laughter like a kangeroo with hiccups. It had been such a clever notion to pop a crab in a hat and leave it for Herman to find!

A crowd of villagers now stood watching

Herman plod steadily after the retreating hat. Then, perhaps because the crab was bored, the hat stopped. Herman reached down, whisked it up, then whisked it away again swiftly when he saw the crab inside. The hat spun away like a dustbin lid and landed behind a bush. Guess who it landed on!

'It's got me! Help, I'm being nipped to death!'

Grump capered from behind the bush and danced around the sand, tearing at the hat wedged onto his head. The crab would not let go. It took three trips around a palm tree and a lot of tugging before the hat flew off, and lumps of Grump's hair went with it.

'Did you see that?' Grump wailed. 'I'm as bald as a bedknob!'

If Grump had not looked so indignant, perhaps nobody would have laughed. But laugh they did, clutching each other and slapping their sides in delight. That's what hurt Grump – the laughter. He had heard it so often before, and suddenly he was the old angry Grump again, blaming poor innocent Herman.

'It's your fault!' he told him. 'You did that on purpose to make me look silly!'

Even when he found that his friends still seemed to like him despite laughing at him, he still could not forgive Herman. He was afraid of losing the happiness he had found, and that made him unkind.

'You always ruin things for me,' he said to Herman. 'Just go away and leave me alone!'

In the end Herman did just that, though without Grump to play with life seemed no fun any more. From then on he spent his days

on the cliff, standing dolefully trunk to trunk with the stone mammoth there. Even Grump felt guilty sometimes when he saw him there.

'But it's not my fault,' he would mutter. 'Nobody asked him to follow me here, anyway.'

From that day on, though, Grump's new home felt spoiled for him. There was something else, too. The villagers seemed uneasy. They spent hours looking at the sea with worried eyes.

'What's wrong?' Grump asked at last. 'Why is everyone upset?'

'It will soon be the time of the big wind,' a man replied. 'The air will screech and the sea will roar.'

Grump felt his hair prickle. 'But . . . we're safe here, aren't we?' he asked.

The man shrugged. 'Who knows? Sometimes a mighty wave comes. It can sweep away this village . . . all of us.'

Grump shuddered. The thought of something terrible happening to the place he had learned to love so much filled him with dread. Now he, too, took to watching the sea uneasily.

When it came, the storm was sudden and terrible. One minute Grump was asleep dreaming of calm days on a gentle sea, and the next he was being shaken awake by a worried friend.

'Quick, we must escape,' the man said. 'A wave is coming – the biggest anyone has ever seen!'

Grump needed no urging. Quicker than a sparrow's blink, he stumbled out to join the other villagers hurrying away inland. The wind and rain battered them as they fled. Grump had never been more scared. It was only then that he remembered Herman.

'The hairy bouncer won't know about the wave!' he gasped.

The strange thing was that Grump did not hesitate. Much as he told himself that he disliked Herman, he found himself turning and struggling against the wind towards the sea. He knew where he would find Herman.

'Come away, you crusty idiot! He can't help you . . . he's only stone!'

Herman was on the clifftop, his ears streaming in the howling wind, staring intently at the stone mammoth. Grump was tugging desperately at his coat, but the mammoth ignored him. Grump looked at the sea. In the distance a wave as tall as a house was charging towards him. It would sweep away the village, for sure, and perhaps themselves!

'Please, Herman,' he pleaded, 'we've got to

go!'

It was when he looked back at Herman that Grump had his idea. For a second he thought that the stone mammoth really was alive. It was actually moving. Then he realised that it was shaking in the wind, and anything that shook could perhaps be pushed over.

'Down there!' He gazed down into the gap between the points of the cliffs. and if we can block that . . .'

Only Grump could have persuaded Herman to do what he did. And only for his caveman chum would the mammoth have destroyed his stone friend. As it was, it needed all of Herman's strength. He put his vast blunt head against the stone mammoth and pushed with all of his mighty strength. Grump glanced at the sea. The wave was almost upon them, filling the whole sky.

'Push! Push harder, Herman!' he cried.

Herman heaved again. The wave was almost at the gap. There was a creak, a crash, and the rock mammoth crashed slowly into the gap just as the wave arrived. The sea churned angrily against the fallen rocks for a moment, and swept harmlessly along the cliff. The village was saved!

'For he's a jolly good caveman,
A really terribly brave man . . .'

The villagers were singing and carrying Grump in triumph. They had returned to their home with the bright clear dawn, and now he was their hero. He should have been happy – he was in a way – yet curiously he was thinking of Herman.

'He's down by the cliff, looking at his stone chum that I made him destroy.'

As soon as he could, Grump slipped away to where, at the foot of the cliff, Herman was quietly looking at the wreckage of the stone mammoth. Grump hesitated, then touched him gently.

'You miss it all, don't you?' he said. 'The

mountains, and the snow, and your real mammoth friends.'

Herman turned his wide dark eyes to Grump, and the caveman knew with an emptiness in his heart that if they stayed here the mammoth would die with loneliness.

'All right,' he whispered, 'if you want to go back I'll take you.'

And so, a week later, Grump said goodbye to the place where he had been so happy. His raft now had a sail so that he could go upstream, and with a mammoth to pull him over the rough places they would make it back to the mountains. Herman was already on the raft, and Grump was about to step aboard when a small girl took his hand shyly.

'Goodbye, Grump,' she said, 'and come back one day. We'll miss you.'

Grump tried to smile bravely. 'Oh, I'll come back,' he said.

But he knew in his secret heart as the raft rounded the bend of the river and the village edged from his sight, that he would never return. He had been happy there, so happy, but you can only visit heaven once . . .

'Goodbye,' he murmured, 'and thank you for liking me.'

Then he turned and looked ahead. In the distance he could see the mountains. He thought of their cold and their snow and the wind that bit in the freezing air. He thought of those things and he should have been unhappy, but he wasn't. His eyes were shining as he touched the warm fur of the great patient animal standing beside him.

'We're going home, Herman,' he whispered, 'we're actually going home!'